Classic Adventures

The Red Badge of Courage

by
Stephen Crane

retold by
John Matern

Don Johnston Incorporated
Volo, Illinois

Edited by:

Jerry Stemach, MS, CCC-SLP
AAC Specialist, Adaptive Technology Center, Sonoma County, California

Gail Portnuff Venable, MS, CCC-SLP
Speech-Language Pathologist, Scottish Rite Center for Childhood Language Disorders, San Francisco, California

Dorothy Tyack, MA
Learning Disabilities Specialist, Scottish Rite Center for Childhood Language Disorders, San Francisco, California

Ted S. Hasselbring, PhD
Professor of Special Education, Vanderbilt University, Nashville, Tennessee

Cover Design and Illustration:
Karyl Shields, Jack Nichols

Interior Illustrations:
Jack Nichols

Published by:
Don Johnston Incorporated
26799 West Commerce Drive
Volo, IL 60073

DON JOHNSTON

International Standard Book Number
ISBN 1-893376-04-4

Contents

Chapter 1
Off to War **1**

Chapter 2
The First Battle **11**

Chapter 3
Dead Men **24**

Chapter 4
The Red Badge **35**

Chapter 5
Brave Soldiers **48**

Chapter 6
The Campfire **56**

Chapter 7
More Bullets **68**

Chapter 8
The Flag **80**

Chapter 9
Real Men **91**

Chapter 10
A Dream of Peace **100**

Chapter 1

Off to War

A tall soldier in a blue uniform ran into camp. The soldier's name was Jim, and he was a private in the army. "We're gonna move!" Jim yelled. "We're gonna move. We're gonna move out tomorrow!" Everyone in the camp stopped to listen to Jim. A black soldier stopped singing. Other men stopped talking.

"That's a darn lie, Jim Conklin!" said one of the men. "We ain't moved in two weeks."

Jim said that he heard about the move from a friend of his.

The friend had heard about it from his brother. The brother had heard about it from someone who was very important in the army. Jim was sure that the soldiers in the 304th regiment were going to move the next day. "We're gonna fight those Rebel soldiers at last," said Jim.

One young soldier—a youth— listened to Jim, too. After Jim spoke, the youth went back to his cabin. The youth and Jim were friends, but right now the youth just wanted to be alone.

He thought about his mother back home on their farm.

The youth went back to his cabin and sat down on his bed. He started to think. He thought about his mother back home on their farm. He thought about the day that he joined the army. His mother had not wanted him to join. She said that he was more important alive on the farm than dead in a war. But the youth wanted to be a hero, so he joined the army anyway. He remembered how his mother became sad when he told her about joining. He remembered the day he left home.

He remembered the girl from his town who also looked sad when he left. He remembered how his mother sent him off to war with eight pairs of socks, clean shirts, and a jar of blackberry jam. Before he left, she said just three things to him. "Watch out," she said. "Do what is right, and be a good boy, Henry."

It was 1861, and the youth went to fight in the Civil War. He dreamed about wearing a blue uniform and fighting for the North in great battles.

He thought that he would be so brave.
But now he was not so sure that he
would be brave in a real fight with
real guns.

Meanwhile, the tall soldier, Jim, was
thinking, too. Jim thought about what
he had done in the army so far.
During the first three months, Jim and
the other soldiers in the regiment had
not done much at all. Most of the time,
they had just sat still and tried to stay
warm at night. Most of the soldiers in
Jim's regiment were new, and they had
never fought in a war before.

In fact, so far they had not even seen one enemy soldier. But tomorrow they would see the enemy. And tomorrow they would fight.

The youth sat in his cabin and thought some more. He thought about fighting. Would he be scared? Would he fight or would he run away? He had never thought about running away before. "What's the matter with me?" he whispered.

Jim came into the youth's cabin. The youth looked up at him and asked him a question.

"Jim," he said. "Are you sure we're gonna fight tomorrow?"

"You bet I'm sure," Jim answered. "You'll see fighting this time!"

"How do you think our regiment will do?" the youth asked.

"I think they'll do OK after they start fighting," Jim answered.

"How do you think you'll do?" the youth asked. "Do you think you might run away?"

"If everyone else ran away, I might run, too," Jim said.

"But if everyone stayed and fought, then I'd stay and fight, too. You can bet on that!"

The youth was still not sure what he would do. Would he run? Or would he fight? He was tired of waiting to find out. He stayed awake all night and worried about it.

Chapter 2

The First Battle

The next morning, the soldiers were up before dawn. They had orders to move. It looked like Jim was right. They were moving toward their first battle. Today they would fight. Most of the soldiers in the 304th regiment were excited. They talked about fighting the enemy at last. They cleaned and loaded their guns.

But the youth did not do any of these things. When the soldiers started to walk, the youth walked way in back of the others. He felt alone. He was still thinking about running away.

The long line of soldiers marched on and on for miles. As the sun got higher in the sky, they became hot and tired. Their feet were sore and they were hungry. Some soldiers threw off their backpacks. Others took off their thick, blue shirts and threw them on the ground. They only carried their guns and water.

The youth walked along and looked at the land around him. He saw the thick, green grass, the tall pine trees and the low hills.

He saw the river going through the woods. "This land is too beautiful for a war," he said.

The youth wished that he and the others could stop walking.
He wished that an enemy soldier would just kill him. That would put an end to his worrying, he thought.
He had too much time now to think.
His legs were so tired that they felt weak. He was sure that he was walking to his death. He wished that he had never joined the army in the first place.

At last, a general on a horse told the soldiers to stop. When they stopped, they saw other troops of soldiers. The soldiers in the other troops were older and they had been in the war a long time. The older soldiers were using rocks and branches from trees to make hiding places. Some were digging holes. The youth and the other soldiers in the 304th regiment watched. Then they built hiding places, too.

After the youth had finished making a hiding place out of rocks and branches, he got behind it.

He peeked out over the top. Then he saw them. Enemy soldiers in grey uniforms were way out across the field in front of the youth. At first he saw little puffs of smoke. Then he heard gun shots. The youth saw bullets hit in the dirt and in the trees a long way off. Some men screamed. When the shooting ended, the youth saw the body of a dead Rebel fighter out in the field.

The man was lying on his back and looking up into the sky with dead eyes. The youth felt a tight lump in his throat.

The general told the regiment to get up and walk again. The soldiers left their hiding places and moved out. Now the youth felt angry. He was tired of waiting to see if he would fight or run. "I can't stand this much longer," he cried.

The regiment was getting closer and closer to the battle.

The youth asked him, "Wilson, how do you think

you'll fight today?"

The noise from guns and big cannons was growing louder.

The youth walked next to a soldier named Wilson. The youth asked him, "Wilson, how do you think you'll fight today?"

"I'll fight as good as the next man," Wilson answered.

"You won't run away, will you?" the youth asked.

"Of course not!" yelled Wilson.

"But how do you know?" the youth asked.

"Cuz I won't, that's why!" Wilson
answered. "Now shut up!"

After another long march, the
regiment was told to stop.
The soldiers built hiding places
again. The youth sat down next to
Wilson. Bullets began to fly right
past them. This time the bullets
were a lot closer. A big gun shell
went just over their heads and
exploded in some trees nearby.
Other soldiers in blue uniforms
went running past.

Wilson took a yellow envelope from his pocket and handed it to the youth.

The youth looked at their faces. "They look plenty scared," he said to Wilson.

Wilson turned to the youth. "Henry," he said. "Do me a favor, will you?"

"What is it?" the youth asked.

Wilson took a yellow envelope from his pocket and handed it to the youth. "Will you make sure that this envelope gets to my family?" he asked.

"This will be my first battle," said Wilson. "And it will be my last battle. I'm gonna die, Henry. I just know it."

The youth took the envelope and put it in his pocket.

Chapter 3

Dead Men

The youth sat in his hiding place next to Wilson. Someone was yelling. "Here they come! Here they come!" The soldiers in the youth's regiment got ready. They loaded their guns and set extra bullets by their side. A general rode his horse behind them and screamed, "You've got to hold 'em back, boys! You've got to hold 'em!"

A man sitting next to the youth shook his head. "We're in for it now," he said.

Suddenly, the youth could not remember if his gun was loaded. He tried to think back, but he could not remember. He began to sweat. He wiped the sweat from his eyes. Then the youth peeked over his hiding place and saw the grey uniforms of the Rebel soldiers. They were running right toward him! They were big men who wore big, grey coats. Their rifles shined through the smoke. The youth stopped thinking about his gun.

The youth fired a wild shot at the enemy soldiers before he was even ready. Then he quickly reloaded his rifle and fired again. The men on each side of him fired their rifles, too. Soon, everyone was shooting. The gun shots were very loud, and smoke filled the air like fog.

The youth forgot about running. There was no time to think at all. He fired his gun, reloaded it, then fired again.

The youth was no longer just Henry Fleming, all by himself.

He was part of something much bigger now. All of the men in his regiment were like one big family. They were all brothers.

The youth was wet with sweat, but his eyes felt like dry, hot stones. Boom! Bang! Loud explosions filled his ears. On the inside, he felt like a trapped animal. He was angry and scared all at the same time. He got mad at his rifle because it could only kill one enemy soldier at a time. He wanted to make all of the enemy soldiers turn around and run away.

The youth stood up and stepped back from his rifle.

When the shooting slowed down, the youth looked up to see that the Rebel soldiers were running away. The 304th regiment had stopped them! "We've held 'em!" someone yelled from down the line of soldiers. The youth stood up and stepped back from his rifle. Slowly, his anger left him. He saw dead men lying on the ground all around him. They looked like they had dropped out of the sky. Then he saw his flag. Its stars and stripes looked bright in the sunshine. Behind the flag, the sky was blue.

The fighting was over at last.

The youth had passed the test!

He had fought in a battle and did

not run away. He felt happy and

he started to relax. Then he heard

someone yell.

"Here they come again! They're

comin' back!" said the voice.

The youth could not believe it.

"I'm having a bad dream," he

thought. But the enemy guns

began to fire again.

The youth picked up his rifle.

"We ain't never gonna last this time!" he said.

But this time it did not feel right in his hands. His fingers felt big and swollen. His arms felt tired and sore. The youth peeked out from his hiding place. He could not believe that the enemy was coming again. "They must be made out of steel," he thought to himself.

One of the soldiers in the youth's regiment was shot. Blood was running down his face. The soldier dropped his rifle and ran. Another soldier yelled. "We ain't never gonna last this time!" he said.

That soldier threw down his gun too. Then he turned and ran off.

The youth could not think clearly. First he dropped his rifle. Then he turned his back to the Rebel army and started to run. He felt his hat fall off, but he did not stop to get it. He ran fast and far. He ran like a blind man and he tripped many times. The youth did not know where he was going. He just kept running.

Chapter 4

The Red Badge

The youth ran across a wide field. Other soldiers were running away, too. Shells from big guns exploded all around him. The youth ran past other troops of soldiers who were still fighting. The youth could not decide if these soldiers were brave, stupid, or crazy. At one point he ran past a general. The general was smiling as he sat on his horse. The general yelled, "We've held 'em back, by heavens! The 304th regiment has held back the Rebel army!"

The youth stopped running. He could not believe what had happened. The youth's regiment had held back the Rebel soldiers again. He felt like he had been tricked. He had run away to save his own life. He had thought that everyone in his regiment was going to die. The other men had seemed like fools because they stayed to fight. Now the other soldiers in his regiment had won the battle, and the youth felt like a fool himself.

The youth was a coward. He had been afraid to stay. But the youth was mad. He felt that running away was the right thing to do. If he had not run, he would be dead by now. He went further and further into the forest. He went into the forest so far that he could no longer hear the noise of the war.

The trees were thick in the forest. The youth went slowly through the long, low branches. He was walking on a soft carpet of pine needles.

The youth wanted to lie down and rest. He found an open spot near a big tree. Then he saw it. Sitting against the tree was the body of a dead soldier. The dead man's eyes were dull and grey. His blue uniform was rotting and turning green. The dead man's mouth was open. His tongue was yellow and ants were crawling across his grey face. The dead man seemed to be looking right at the youth. The youth stood still and stared.

At last, the youth turned and ran. He ran away from the tree and out of the forest. As he ran, he looked behind him. He was sure that the dead man would try to follow him.

When he got out of the forest, the youth could hear the sounds of another, bigger battle. He walked along a road toward the sounds. He came to a group of wounded soldiers. They all limped along like a sad parade of bloody men. One soldier had a shoe full of blood.

One screamed in pain and held his bloody hand against his head. Others were moaning and cussing. They were hurt in all different ways. The youth walked down the dusty road with them.

One of the wounded men spoke to the youth. "We fought pretty good, didn't we?" said the man. The youth did not answer him. The wounded man tried again. "It was a pretty good fight, wasn't it?" The youth looked over at the beat up man.

The blood looked like a badge that the man had gotten for fighting.

His head was bleeding and his arm

was badly hurt. There were spots

of red blood on the man's blue shirt.

The blood looked like a badge that

the man had gotten for fighting.

It was a red badge of courage,

thought the youth. The wounded

man looked over at the youth.

"Where did you get hit?" he asked.

The youth looked down at the road.

Then he turned away and quickly left

the wounded soldier. The youth

walked to the back of the group.

He wished that he was wounded, too.

"If I was wounded," he said, "I would be happy." The youth wanted his own red badge of courage.

Then the youth had a shock. He saw his old friend Jim, the tall soldier from the 304th regiment. Jim was bleeding badly from his side. He looked white and weak and close to death. The youth ran over to him. "Jim! Oh, Jim!" he yelled.

"Henry? Is that you?" Jim said. "It sure is good to see ya, Henry. I thought you was dead for sure," said Jim.

He looked white and weak and close to death.

The youth tried to help Jim, but Jim would not let him. "I got myself shot," said Jim. "Now you just leave me be, Henry," he said. "Just leave me be."

The youth tried to speak to his friend. But the youth was crying inside, and his words were stuck in his throat. Jim was dying! The youth saw his friend stagger off the road and into a field. Jim held his bloody side. He stood straight up. Then Jim fell over like a great tall tree.

He crashed to the ground with a thud. The youth looked at Jim and then back toward the battle field. He raised his fist and screamed, "HELL!...."

Chapter 5

Brave Soldiers

The youth went over to Jim and stood by him. The youth wanted to scream. His friend, Jim, was dead. One of the wounded soldiers came up to the youth. The wounded soldier spoke. "It's time to move on. No one can bother Jim any more," he said. "You gotta look out for your own self now."

The youth and the wounded man walked together for a while. The wounded man began to talk again. "We was fightin' this afternoon.

And, all of a sudden, my buddy, Tom, yelled that I was shot. My head was all bloody and I didn't even know it. Tom made me stop fighting."

The youth did not say anything, but the wounded man kept on talking.

"Good old Tom," he said.

The wounded man talked, but he did not make any sense.

The youth looked at the man. He was bleeding from his head and his arm. His skin looked white. The wounded man seemed to think that the youth was his buddy, Tom.

"Tom," said the man. "Tom, where did you get hit, old buddy?"

The youth started to walk away. "Don't bother me!" he answered.

The wounded man called after him. "Now where are you goin'?"

The youth pointed toward the battle noises. "Over there," he said. As he walked, he watched another troop of soldiers who were going into battle. "What makes them so brave?" the youth asked himself.

"What do those soldiers eat that makes them so brave?"

The youth thought about being with these soldiers. He thought about being brave like them. The youth thought about fighting to his death in a battle. He thought about leading other soldiers against the Rebel army. These thoughts made the youth feel excited. "Yes!" he said to himself. "I will fight again!"

Then the youth stopped.

He remembered that he did not have

a rifle anymore. He did not even

know where the 304th regiment was.

But these were just excuses.

The youth could join this troop of

soldiers if he wanted to. There were

plenty of guns that were left along

the road next to dead soldiers.

The youth began to hate himself

again. He felt tired and sore.

He felt hungry and thirsty.

How could he fight when he felt like

this?

He could not go back to his own regiment now. The soldiers in his regiment would all hate him.

They would know that he had run away. The other soldiers would talk about him behind his back.

They would laugh and say, "Didn't Henry Fleming run away?"

The youth wished again that his army would lose the war. Then he could go back. Then the soldiers would think that the youth was smart to run. But the army kept winning every battle!

The brave soldiers held back the enemy every time. The youth was just a coward. The youth wished that he was one of the dead soldiers. They were the lucky ones. Even if they had been cowards, too, now they were dead. They didn't have to worry any more about feeling afraid. And people back home would always think that they had been brave.

Chapter 6

The Campfire

The youth walked up a hill. All of a sudden, he saw hundreds of soldiers in blue jackets running out of the woods and into a field. Behind them, the youth could see smoke and red explosions. Soon the men were all around him. The youth turned to look at them. They looked scared. The soldiers were running like crazy people. The youth could tell that these men had just lost their battle. The youth saw that these soldiers were not from his regiment.

The man swung his rifle and hit the youth over the head with it.

He tried to speak to them, but they ran right past him. Finally, the youth grabbed one of the men by the arm.

"What happened?" the youth started to ask.

"Let go of me!" the man screamed. "Let go of me!"

The youth did not let go. He tried again. "Why are you running?"

"All right then," the man said. The man swung his rifle and hit the youth over the head with it. Then the man ran away.

The youth fell to the ground with a thud. His head pounded. He tried to get up, but he sank back down again. The pain in his head felt like thunder. The youth crawled on his hands and knees. He touched his head with his hand. He was bleeding badly. The youth was dizzy, but at last he stood up. He could still hear the noise of the big guns behind him. "I can't stop here," he said. "I can't stop."

The youth made himself walk. He tried to keep his head still.

He tried to think about other things.

He thought about his mom and the

good meals that she made.

He remembered swimming in a cool

pond with his friends. The youth

grew very tired and he wanted to lie

down. "No," he said to himself.

"Not safe." So the youth just kept

walking one step at a time.

It was nighttime now. The youth

was walking slowly so that he would

not trip and fall. Suddenly he heard

a voice behind him.

A man held the youth's arm and they stumbled

along together.

"You seem to be in a pretty bad way, boy," a friendly voice said. The youth just grunted. "I guess I could walk with ya for a bit," the voice said.
A man held the youth's arm and they stumbled along together. The youth told about the 304th regiment from New York. The friendly man knew where the regiment was. He and the youth walked for many hours back to find it.

At last the friendly man pointed to a campfire. "You see that fire right over there?" he asked.

"That's the 304th." Then the man left. The youth had never even seen his face.

The youth went slowly up to the fire. He was too tired to think of any lies to tell the troops. He was too tired and too hungry. When he got close to the fire, he saw a huge man there. The man was pointing a gun at the youth.

"Halt! Halt!" the man yelled. It was good old Wilson, the loud private! Wilson looked at the youth. "Henry?" he asked. "Is that you?

I sure am glad to see ya," said Wilson.
"Boy, I thought you was dead," he
said.

"It's me," the youth said. "I've had
a bad time. I been way over there with
Jim Conklin." He pointed into the
darkness behind him. "Jim is dead,"
he said. Then he told a lie. "I got shot
in the head. I ain't feeling so good."

"You hurt?" Wilson asked.
"Why didn't you say so?" Wilson took
the youth over to the fire and looked
at his head. "It looks like you was
grazed by a bullet," he said.

"It looks like you was grazed by a bullet," he said.

"But I'll fix you up." Wilson put

a bandage on the youth's head.

Then he gave him some coffee.

The youth drank and drank.

His throat was very dry. Wilson

put the youth into his own bed.

The bed felt very soft. As the

youth fell into a deep sleep, he

heard gunshots far away.

"Do those Rebs ever sleep?"

he asked.

Chapter 7

More Bullets

The youth woke up before dawn. He felt like he had been sleeping for a thousand years. His head felt like a big watermelon. He looked around. Soldiers were still asleep all around him. He could hear the crackle of a small campfire.

Wilson saw that the youth was awake, so he went over to him. "Well, Henry ol' man," said Wilson. "How are you feelin' this mornin'?" he asked.

"Thunder!" the youth answered. "I still feel pretty bad."

Wilson told the youth about the other soldiers in the 304th regiment.

Wilson looked at the youth's head.
He fixed the bandage again.
But when Wilson fixed the bandage,
the youth felt a sharp pain. It felt
like Wilson was pounding nails into
the youth's head. Wilson brought
a plate of food and a cup of coffee.

Wilson told the youth about the
other soldiers in the 304th regiment.
"They were lost, too," he said.
"Just like you. We thought they was
all dead. But they keep comin' back."

"So what?" said the youth.
He did not want to talk about it.

While the youth was eating, three men started fighting. Wilson went over to stop them. The youth looked at Wilson. Was this the same Wilson? Just a few days before, Wilson had acted like a loud, selfish child. He had acted like a person who did not think about others. Now Wilson had become a very kind and wise man.

The youth could hear someone playing a bugle. Every soldier in the regiment woke up. They were all stiff and sore.

They got up, ate breakfast, and waited for their orders. The youth was standing by Wilson.

Then the youth remembered something. He still had Wilson's envelope in his pocket that Wilson had given to him before the first battle! He remembered that Wilson had been afraid to die. The youth decided not to give it back.

If anybody asked him about running away, he could tell them about Wilson and the envelope.

The youth reached slowly into his pocket and got

out the envelope.

But Wilson remembered about the envelope too.

"Henry," Wilson said. "You can give me those letters now."
The youth reached slowly into his pocket and got out the envelope. He wanted to say something funny. He wanted to tease Wilson about it first. But the youth decided to be kind. He handed it to Wilson and said nothing.

Soon, the 304th regiment was given the order to move out.

The soldiers all started to march toward the battle. The noise of explosions grew louder and louder. The youth's regiment was sent to take the place of another regiment. Now the soldiers in the 304th regiment hid in a ditch and waited for the enemy. They waited for the enemy to shoot at them. After a long wait, some of the soldiers in the 304th regiment became angry. They complained to each other.

The youth spoke up. "Good Gawd," the youth said.

"We're always bein' chased around like rats! We're just like sittin' ducks for the Rebel soldiers. It makes me sick!" Other soldiers agreed with the youth. They began to grumble and swear at the leaders.

The captain yelled back at all of them. "You boys shut up! All you have to do is fight! I want to see less talkin' and more fightin'. And in ten minutes or less, you'll have your chance to fight!"

Soon the enemy soldiers came closer.

He lifted his gun and took aim.

Enemy bullets flew over the heads of the soldiers in the 304th regiment. Other regiments joined the 304th until they had formed a long, blue line. The youth saw a rifle flash in the distance. Little puffs of smoke began to fill the air. Soon the noise of the guns sounded like thunder. The soldiers in the 304th looked at each other. They were tired and sore. The youth looked out at the Rebel army. He lifted his gun and took aim.

Chapter 8

The Flag

As he aimed at the enemy soldiers, the youth became more and more angry. He thought that the enemy soldiers did not have any feelings. "They are hunters who have no feelings about anything," he said to himself. The youth wanted more time to think about what had happened the day before. But the enemy soldiers would not give him time to think about yesterday. The youth wanted time to rest. But the enemy soldiers would not give him time to rest.

Instead, the line of enemy soldiers came closer and closer. The youth felt like a cat trapped in a corner. "I can't take much more of this!" the youth cried. "They better look out!"

Then the real fighting began. Cannon fire shook the ground. The youth forgot about everything except the battle. He stood up tall and fired at the Rebels. He reloaded, aimed, and pulled the trigger. His rifle was hot and it burned his hands.

He moved right up to the front of the line and faced the enemy soldiers. "The enemy ain't gonna push us into the river," he thought.

After a long battle, the Rebel soldiers turned back. When the fighting stopped, the youth kept on shooting. He stayed in the front of the line and just kept shooting into the smoke.

The other soldiers stopped and looked at him. Someone yelled at the youth.

"You fool! You don't even know
to stop when there ain't nothin' to
shoot at."

The captain came over to the
youth. The captain was very proud
of him. "By heavens!" said the
captain. "If I had ten thousand men
like you, I'd beat them Rebels in a
week."

The youth had become a wild
animal. One soldier came up to him.
"Are you OK, Henry?" he asked.

The youth looked around. All of the other soldiers were staring at him. The youth choked a little. "I'm OK," he said.

The captain sent the youth and Wilson off to get water. On their way back, they saw two generals talking. Wilson and the youth slowed down so that they could hear the generals.

"We need help or the enemy will beat us for sure," one general said to the other. "Who can you send to help us?"

On their way back, they saw two generals talking.

"The 304th is all that's left," the other general answered. "They don't fight hard. They're just a bunch of mud diggers."

"It's all we got," said the first general. "Get them ready to fight in five minutes. I want them to go across the field and charge the enemy," he said. "But you're gonna lose those mud diggers. I don't think that very many men will make it back alive."

Wilson and the youth ran back to the soldiers in their regiment. They told the others what they had heard.

One man looked across the field that they would charge. "Them Rebels will chew us up and spit us out," he said.

The 304th regiment charged anyway. The youth put his head down and ran right at the enemy. Men were being shot all around him. They were falling and screaming. The youth only ran faster. The enemy shot at the soldiers until most of them stopped running. But when they slowed down, more of them got shot. The youth ran into the clouds of smoke at top speed.

The youth could see one of the soldiers in his regiment who was carrying their flag. The youth loved this flag. It gave him hope. It was like a powerful goddess. The youth wanted to stay near it. But then, the man with the flag was shot. He fell slowly to the ground. The youth ran to the man and the flag. The man was dead. The youth grabbed the flag. "Someone has to carry our flag," he said.

He knew that he could not carry the flag and his rifle at the same time. Wilson ran up to him and grabbed the flag. Both men wanted to carry it.

Chapter 9

Real Men

Wilson put his hand out to take the flag. "Give it to me," he yelled.

"No, I'll take it," the youth yelled back. The youth knew that Wilson could carry the flag just fine. And Wilson knew that the youth could carry it just as well. They both felt it was a great honor to carry the flag. At last the youth grabbed the flag and pushed Wilson away from it.

The youth looked around at the soldiers in his regiment.

The Rebels were still shooting at them. The men who did not get hit turned and ran back to safety. Wilson and the youth ran after them.

"Stop!" yelled the youth. "We must fight!"

But these soldiers felt beaten. Many were wounded. Many others had been killed. Now, for one minute, there were no bullets flying at their heads. There were no generals screaming orders at them. Then the minute was up, and a man yelled. "Here they come, by Gawd!" he said.

Another troop of Rebel soldiers
was coming right at them through the
woods. But these Rebel soldiers were
surprised too. They did not know that
the youth's regiment was also in the
woods. The Rebels were so close that
the youth could see the buttons on
their bright grey uniforms.

The two armies began shooting.
Wilson and the youth went right up
to the front of the line. The gunfire
made a huge cloud of smoke.
The youth was proud of his regiment.

If they were going to die, at least they were going to die with a fight. When the shooting slowed down, the smoke lifted. Bodies of dead Rebel soldiers lay on the ground. The rest of the Rebels were gone! The 304th regiment had won! There were yells and cheers. Every soldier felt proud. They felt like real men.

Wilson and the youth sat and rested. They had both fought well. Other men from the regiment hurried over to them with good news.

"We just heard the general talkin' about you two.

"Henry Fleming!" one of them said. "You should have heard it."

"And you, too, Wilson," another man said. "We just heard the general talkin' about you two.
He was real proud of you two.
He said that you were the best kind of soldier! He said it, sure."

Another man added, "That's right, boys. The general said that you two should be major-generals!"

Wilson and the youth were thrilled.

When it came time to fight again,
they were both very brave. The 304th
regiment charged the Rebels again.
And again, Wilson and the youth were
in the very front. The youth held the
flag high and Wilson fought like a
tiger.

The Rebel soldiers hid safely
behind a wood fence and shot at
the youth's regiment. A Rebel bullet
hit one soldier in the face, and blood
spilled from his mouth. Men on both
sides of the youth were getting hit
by the Rebel gunfire.

The youth stood with the flag on a small hill. He decided that he would not move from there. He would die before he would run away. He would show the general that he was not a mud digger. He looked back and saw Wilson. Wilson nodded back at him. The youth knew that Wilson would not run either.

Chapter 10

A Dream of Peace

The General rode his horse behind the youth's regiment. He screamed at them. "We must charge 'em! We have to charge 'em at the fence!"

The youth thought for a moment. They would die if they stayed where they were. The enemy could hide behind the fence until every last man in the 304th regiment was shot. "Yes," said the youth. "The general is right. But the soldiers are too tired to charge the Rebels." The youth decided to lead the charge.

The youth looked down at his regiment. He could not believe what he saw! The soldiers did not look tired at all. They jumped up. They yelled. The 304th regiment ran forward and charged. The roar of their guns filled the air.

The youth led the way. He kept the flag out in the front. He was sure that the enemy would shoot them all. Smoke and fire came from the guns along the fence. The youth looked.

The soldiers in blue were not
falling. They were moving closer
to the Rebels. The charge was
working. As they got closer, the
youth saw that some of the enemy
soldiers were running away.

The youth's regiment was at the
fence. One Rebel soldier was
waving his own red flag.
The youth wanted to take that
flag away. The men in the youth's
regiment fought like madmen.
They were still shooting.

The youth saw that the man who was holding the enemy flag had been shot. Now Wilson was running to take the flag from the dying man. Wilson grabbed the hated, red flag and held it high over his head. He cheered like a wild man. He waved the flag back and forth. The 304th regiment had won.

The youth's regiment took four enemy soldiers as prisoners. Then the regiment was told to head back. They were going back to the river where they had started.

There would not be any fighting there. "It's all over," one man said to the youth.

"By Gawd, it is over," the youth agreed.

It started to rain. The youth walked along the muddy road. At last, he had time to think. He was happy that he had been in a great battle and lived. But he thought about other things, too. He remembered how he had run away after his first battle.

He remembered how he left a wounded man to die.

These thoughts made him feel sad.

Then he thought about how he had fought that day. He knew now that he would never be afraid again. He could do anything that the general asked him to do. These thoughts made him feel better.

One thing became very clear to the youth. He would no longer dream of battles. He did not wish to fight again.

Over the river, he saw a bright ray of sunshine come through the rain clouds.

War was a red sickness. And the youth did not want that kind of sickness again. Now, he would dream of blue skies and cool rivers. Now he would dream of peace.

The youth looked up. Over the river, he saw a bright ray of sunshine come through the rain clouds.

The End

A Note from the Start-to-Finish Editors

This book has been divided into approximately equal short chapters so that the student can read a chapter and take the cloze test in one reading session. This length constraint has sometimes required the authors to make transitions in mid-chapter or to break up chapters in unexpected places.

Some content change is inevitable in order to retell a 400-page book in less than 8000 words. The authors have had to eliminate some characters and incidents and sometimes manipulate the story's sequence to produce a cohesive story. Every attempt has been made to maintain the essence of the plot, characters, and style of the book.

You will also notice that Start-to-Finish Books look different from other high-low readers and chapter books. The text layout of this book coordinates with the other media components (CD and audiocassette) of the Start-to-Finish series.

The text in the book matches, line-for-line and page-for-page, the text shown on the computer screen, enabling readers to follow along easily in the book. Each page ends in a complete sentence so that the student can either practice the page (repeat reading) or turn the page to continue with the story. If the next sentence cannot fit on the page in its entirety, it has been shifted to the next page. For this reason, the sentence at the top of a page may not be indented, signaling that it is part of the paragraph from the preceding page.

Words are not hyphenated at the ends of lines. This sometimes creates extra space at the end of a line, but eliminates confusion for the struggling reader.